The return of OLD SMOKEY

story by Valerie King
pictures by Colin King

The Colne Valley Railway was closed long ago;
The steam trains were dirty and travelled too slow.

They shut up the stations and took down the signs,
and thought it was clever to close all the lines.

The railway officials arrived for the day,
and Smokey the steam train was taken away.

Old driver Fred sadly took off his cap;
he watched as his best friend was taken for scrap.

A large bossy diesel with bright shiny chain,
bullied and whined at the smokey old train.

Through fields and strange places it pulled very hard,
and rattled along to the lonely scrapyard.

There in the long grass and tangle of wood,
cold and forgotten the broken trains stood.
They stared as Old Smokey the steam train passed by,
then with creaking and groaning they started to cry.

'Once we were polished and thought we were grand,
we were kings of the railways all over the land.
We called at smart stations and left them on time,
now there's nothing for us at the end of the line!'

The years rolled on by and Smokey grew rusty,
his paintwork was peeling, his levers were dusty.
Creepers and flowers climbed round his old dome,
and inside his cab, the birds made their home.

One day a tired traveller came into the yard;
he pulled at his beard and he thought very hard.
'This old engine cab will make me a bed,
there's a space for my feet and a place for my head!'

'I'm cold,' said the man as he looked for some coal,
then he threw some large lumps inside the black hole.
'I'll have a nice rest here,' he said with a smile
and then settled down to sleep for a while.

He was dreaming of bacon, eggs, chips and beans,
hot milky tea and far away scenes.
He suddenly awoke to a sound like a kettle
and hissing of steam and clanking of metal.

Smokey the steam train puffed smoke all around;
the young man just beamed as he jumped to the ground.
Pistons and levers all moved to and fro,
and Smokey set off with his fire all aglow.

He soon met a signal, a very cross fellow.
'You can't come through here' he said with a bellow.
'I've got to keep moving ,' replied the old train;
'I'll never go back to the scrapyard again.'

Around the next bend was a black gloomy tunnel;
the rusty old engine puffed sparks from his funnel.
And in the dim lights strange shapes seemed to glow-
they were ghostly old trains that were lost long ago.

'Don't leave us, don't leave us' he heard the ghosts moan.
'It's not very nice to be here on our own.'
But Smokey the steam train just puffed on his way.
At the end of the tunnel he saw light of day.

Smokey steamed on through the quiet of the night,
racing the clouds in the frosty moonlight.
His fire burnt so low that he ran out of puff,
so he stopped near a house and rumbled, 'OH HUFF!'

Old driver Fred who was snoring in bed,
woke up with a fright. 'Who's there?' he said.
'I think it's a train,' he heard his wife say,
so he followed her out of the house straight away.

'It's Smokey my steam train' said Fred with delight.
'How did he get here at this time of night?'
'This really is strange, it's never been known,
for a steam train to travel along on its own.'

Next day the good news had spread far and wide;
they photographed Fred who was smiling with pride.
A man from the scrapyard said Smokey could stay
and wished him good luck, then bid Fred good-day.

A meeting was held and the Mayoress declared,
that the old railway line was being repaired.
Smokey the steam train was polished and cleaned.
The paint on his boiler now sparkled and gleamed.

The Colne Valley Railway is open again
and Fred is now working aboard his steam train.
They've rebuilt the station and worked very hard,
and they've rescued more trains from the lonely scrapyard.

People buy tickets for rides down the track,
this way and that way, clickerty clack.
The guard blows his whistle, the signal says go,
'Steam trains are magic,' shouts Fred. Did YOU know?